LOUDMOUSE

LOUDMOUSE

Richard Wilbur

Illustrated by
Don Almquist

DOVER PUBLICATIONS, INC.
Mineola, New York

Bibliographical Note

This Dover edition, first published in 2015, is an unabridged republication of the work originally published in the series "A Modern Masters Book for Children" by The Crowell-Collier Press, New York, in 1963.

Library of Congress Cataloging-in-Publication Data

Wilbur, Richard, 1921–
    Loudmouse / Richard Wilbur ; illustrated by Don Almquist.
        pages cm
    "This Dover edition...is an unabridged republication of the work originally published by The Crowell-Collier Press, New York, in 1963"—Copyright page.
    Summary: A mouse with a big voice saves his family from a mouse trap and a cat and prevents the household valuables from being burgled.
    ISBN-13: 978-0-486-79807-3 (paperback)
    ISBN-10: 0-486-79807-0
    [1. Mice—Fiction.] I. Almquist, Don, illustrator. II. Title.
PZ7.W6422Lo 2015
[E]—dc23

                                                                2015013105

Manufactured in the United States by LSC Communications
4500054424
www.doverpublications.com

Once there was a mother mouse
who had four little baby mice.

The four little mice and their mother
lived in the house of Mr. and Mrs. Arthur L. Dowd.

Mr. and Mrs. Dowd lived in the rooms of the house,
and the little mice and their mother lived inside the walls.

One day, the mother mouse thought that the time had come for a talk with her children.

"Children," she said, "you are big little mice now, and I think you are ready to be on your own, and go where you like, and find your own food.

"But first let me tell you some things to remember.
Mr. Dowd does not know that we live in his house, and if
he found out, he would not like it. You must always
take care not to be seen. When you're hungry and want to
visit the kitchen, wait until night when Mr. Dowd is
asleep. And don't leave any tracks on the kitchen floor.
And above all, never make any noise.

A House is not a House without a Mouse

"Do you hear me?"

"I hear you, Mamma,"
  said the first little mouse.

"I hear you, Mamma,"
  said the second little mouse.

"I hear you, Mamma,"
  said the third little mouse.

I HEAR YOU, MAMMA!

said the fourth little mouse,
very loudly.

"Be quiet, child!"
said the mother mouse.
"Yes, be quiet, you loud mouse!"
said the other little mice.
And Loudmouse was his name, from that time on.

"Loudmouse," said his mother, "just you listen to me.
You must not talk in that bad loud way,
because if you do,
Mr. Dowd will hear you.

"And if he hears you, he will know that there are mice in his house, and he will go and buy a mousetrap or a cat."

A MOUSETRAP?

said Loudmouse, very loudly.

WHAT'S THAT?

"Be quiet, child!" said his mother. "Now, listen to me, and I'll teach you a little song about traps, so that you will always remember what they are."

The little mice sat still and listened while their mother very quietly sang them this song:

If you see a thing
That's a piece of wood
And a kind of a spring
And a hook and a bar
And a bite of cheese
That looks very good,
Don't touch it, please.
Stay where you are.
Take care or—*snap!*—
You'll be caught in a *trap!*

"Now do you know what a trap is like?"
asked the mother mouse.

"Yes, Mamma," said the three quiet little mice.

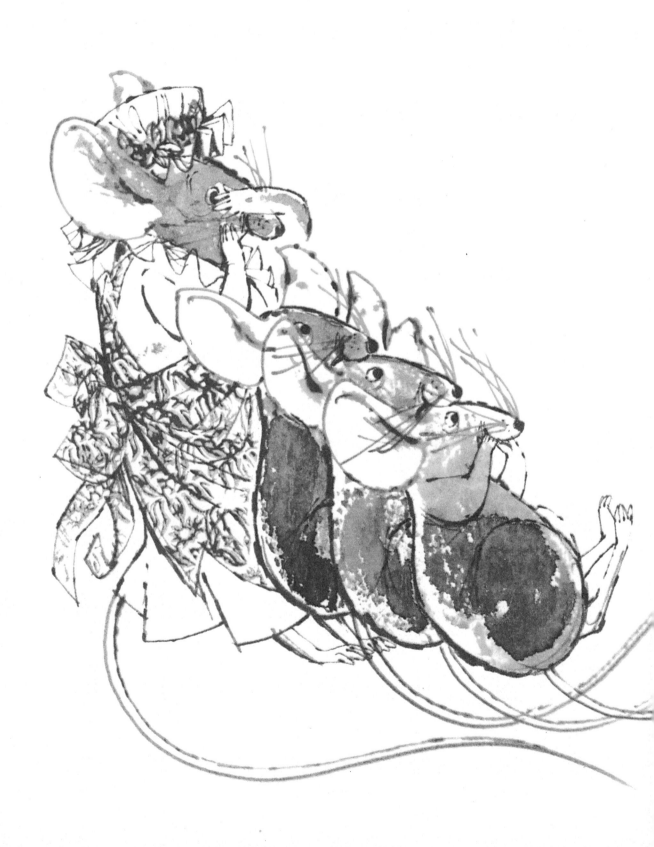

YES, MAMMA!

said Loudmouse, very loudly.

BUT WHAT IS A CAT?

"Be quiet, child!" said his mother.
"Now, listen again, and I'll teach you
a little song about cats, so that
you will never forget what a cat is like."

The little mice sat still and listened while
the mother mouse very quietly sang them this song:

If you see a thing
With eyes that glow
Which looks as though
It's about to spring,
And if it's furry
And has four paws
And a tail, and claws,
And a face that's fat,
Leave in a hurry!
That is a *cat!*

"Now do you know what a cat is like?"
asked the mother mouse.

"Yes, Mamma," said the three quiet little mice.

Yes, Mamma!

said Loudmouse, very loudly.

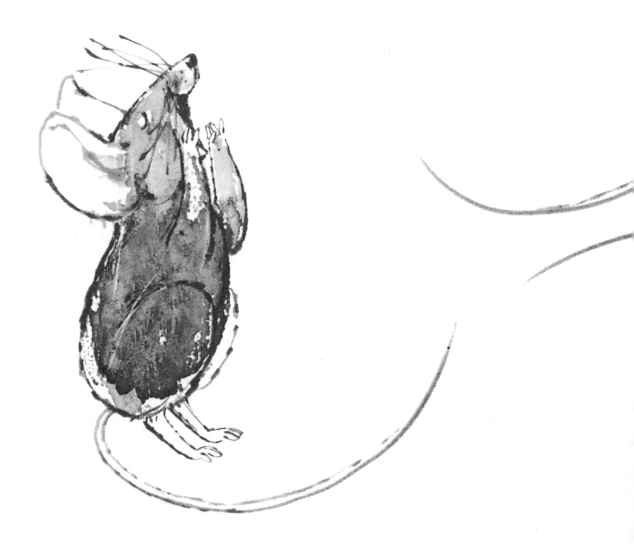

"Be quiet!" everybody told him.

But Loudmouse could not learn to talk in a quiet way.
He wanted to be nice and do what his mother told him, but
every time he said anything, he made a great big noise.

One night, Mr. and Mrs. Dowd
were sitting in the living room,
and Mr. Dowd said,
"Jane, I think there must be
a lion in that wall."

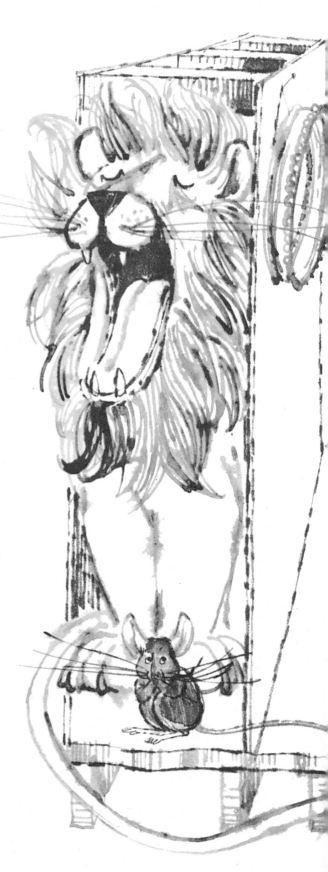

"A lion, dear?"
said Mrs. Dowd.
"Oh, you're just being funny.
There isn't room for a lion
inside that wall."

"Well," said Mr. Dowd,
"something inside that wall
just made a very loud noise.
Didn't you hear it?"

"Come to think of it," said Mrs. Dowd, "I *have* been
hearing noises in this house for about a week.
But I told myself that I must be dreaming."

Just then, Loudmouse said something inside the wall.
He talked so loudly that
it almost made
the house
fall down.

"Really!" said Mrs. Dowd. "We must do something about this."

"I'm pretty sure that it's
just a mouse,"
said Mr. Dowd.
"But I must say
it's a very
loud mouse."

"Please remember
to buy a mousetrap tomorrow,"
said Mrs. Dowd.
"I guess I shall have to," said Mr. Dowd.
"I really like mice, but I don't see how
we can put up with so much noise."

The next night, when Mr. and Mrs. Dowd had gone to bed, Loudmouse was hungry. "I think I'll go to the kitchen," he said to himself,  "and eat some of that fine cheese which Mrs. Dowd has just bought." He stuck his head out of a hole in the living room wall, and looked around to be sure that everybody was gone. On the floor, not far away from the hole, sat a trap with a nice piece of cheese in it. Loudmouse didn't know what it was.

"My, my," he said to himself, "what a pretty piece of cheese."

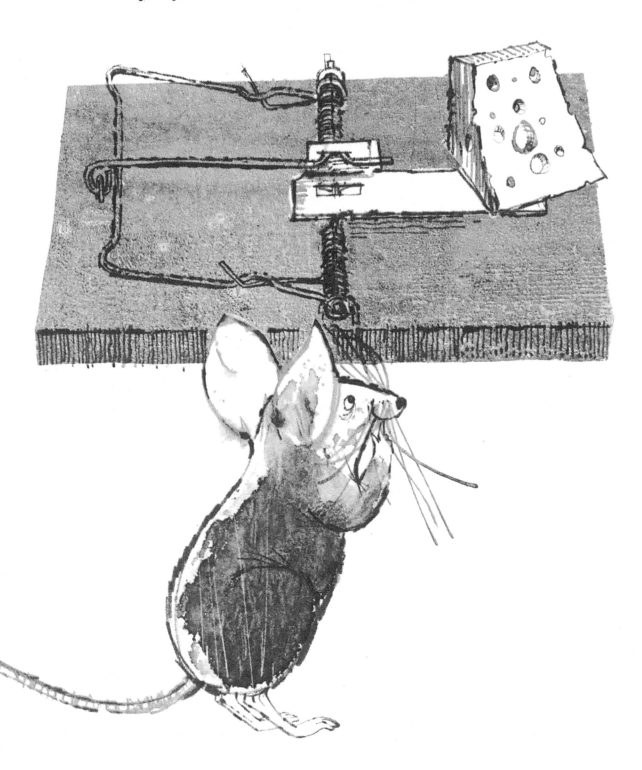

Loudmouse came out of the hole in the wall, and walked over to the trap, and started to take a bite of the cheese. But then something made him stop and think.

He looked hard at the trap, and remembered
his mother's song. He sang the song to himself:

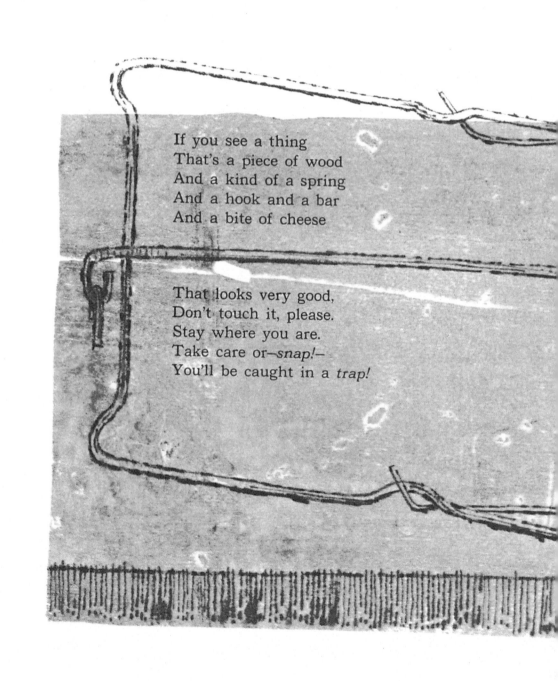

If you see a thing
That's a piece of wood
And a kind of a spring
And a hook and a bar
And a bite of cheese

That looks very good,
Don't touch it, please.
Stay where you are.
Take care or—*snap!*—
You'll be caught in a *trap!*

OH!

said Loudmouse,

as loudly as always, and jumped back from the trap.

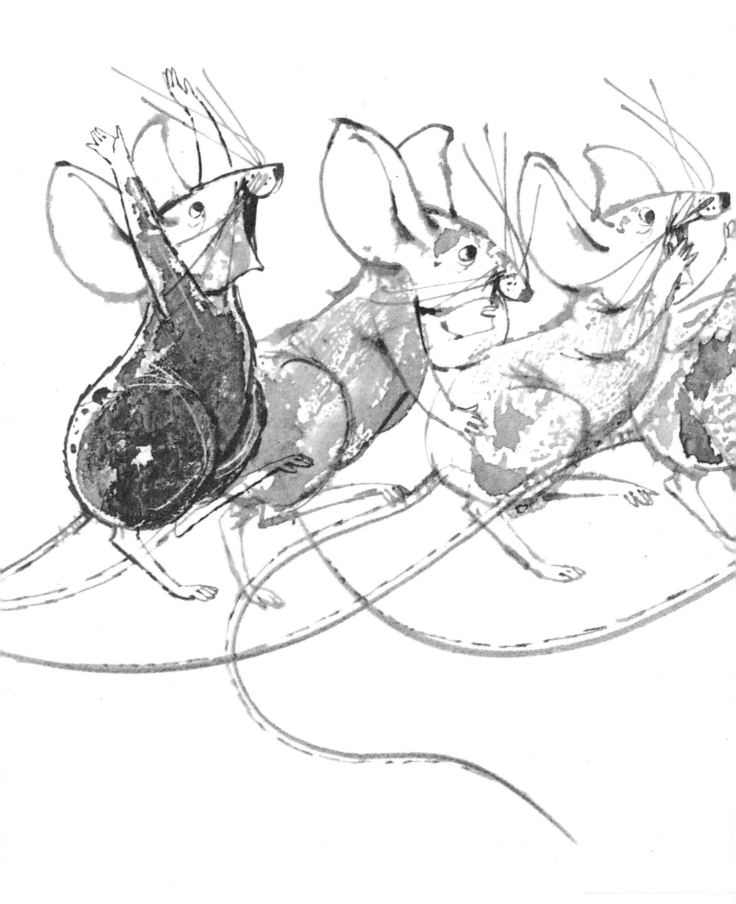

IT'S A TRAP! A TRAP!

A Bad, Bad Trap!

Mr. Dowd heard the noise, got out of bed,
and ran down to the first floor.

He was just in time to see Loudmouse hop back
into his hole, calling loudly to his family.

WATCH OUT, WATCH OUT!

called Loudmouse.

THERE'S A BAD, BAD TRAP IN THE LIVING ROOM!

Mr. Dowd went back to bed and said to Mrs. Dowd, "Jane, that loud animal is a mouse, all right. But I don't think we can catch him in that trap. He knows what it is, and he has just gone to tell his whole family about it."

"Well, said Mrs. Dowd, "there is only one thing to do. You must go to the pet shop tomorrow and buy a cat."

"I guess I'll have to," said Mr. Dowd, "because we really can't put up with all this noise."

The next night, when Mr. and Mrs. Dowd had gone to bed, Loudmouse was hungry again.

He said to himself, "I could do with a bite of that fine cheese in the kitchen.'"

So he stuck his head out of the hole in the living room wall, and looked all around. He was happy to see that the trap was gone. But in its place there was something else, something bigger.

It was a cat.

Loudmouse didn't know that the cat was a cat, and he wanted
to find out what kind of thing it was.
So he came out of the hole in the wall,
and walked right up to where the cat
was sitting. He was about
to say hello, but then something
made him stop and think.
He didn't like the look
on the cat's fat face,
and the words of his
mother's song started
to come back to him.

He sang to himself:

If you see a thing
With eyes that glow
Which looks as though
It's about to spring,
And if it's furry
And has four paws
And a tail, and claws,
And a face that's fat,
Leave in a hurry!
That is a *cat!*

HELP!

said Loudmouse, very loudly.

IT'S A CAT! A CAT!
A BAD, BAD CAT!

That cat was so surprised to hear a mouse make so much
noise that it jumped into the air, fell on its back,
and then ran away as fast as it could go.

Mr. Dowd got out of bed and came downstairs
just in time to see Loudmouse hop back into his hole,
calling loudly to his family.

WATCH OUT, EVERYBODY!

called Loudmouse.

THERE'S A BAD, BAD CAT in THE LIVING ROOM!

The cat was hiding under a chair,
holding its front paws over its ears.

Mr. Dowd went back to bed and said to Mrs. Dowd,
"Jane, that cat is not going to be of much help to us.
It was so surprised to hear so big a noise from a mouse
that now it is afraid of mice. Tomorrow morning,
I shall take the cat back to the pet shop."

"But what are we going to do?" asked Mrs. Dowd. "We can't put up with all this noise."

"I, for one, am going to sleep," said Mr. Dowd.

The next night, when Mr. and Mrs. Dowd had gone to bed, Loudmouse was very hungry. After all, he had not had anything to eat for three days.

"I really must have some of that fine cheese in the kitchen," he said to himself.

So he stuck his head out of the hole in the living room wall, and looked all around. He was glad to see that there was no trap waiting for him, and no cat.

But just at that minute a funny thing happened.

The living room window was quietly opened from the outside, and a man climbed into the room. He was a bad-looking man with a cap on his head and a bag on his back. He walked across the floor without making any noise at all.

He was as quiet as a mouse—as quiet as *most* mice, anyway. At first, Loudmouse could not guess what the man was up to, because he had never seen a robber before.

The robber turned on a light in the
living room and started taking things.

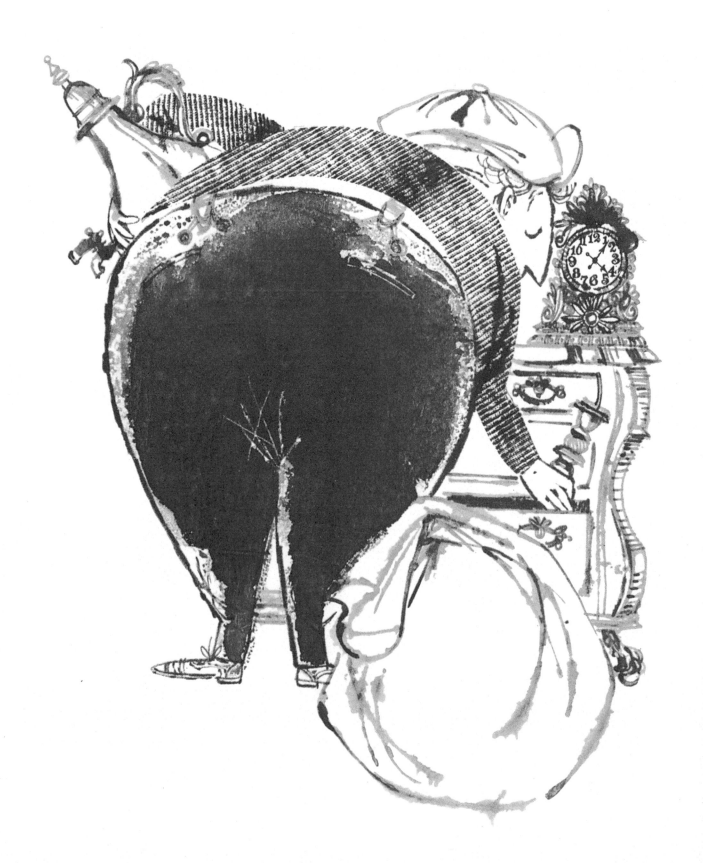

He took a gold box
from an end table
and put it
into his bag.
Then he took
the candlesticks from
above the fireplace,
and put them
into his bag, too.

Loudmouse watched
what the man was doing,
and said to himself,
"There's something
not right about this.
I really don't think
he should be taking
all those things."

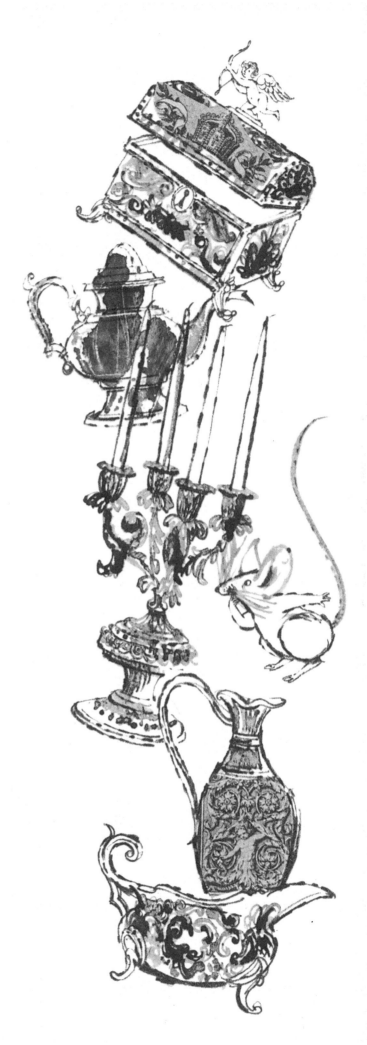

After a while, the robber carried his bag into the next room, and Loudmouse went along, keeping an eye on him. The man looked into all kinds of places and took all kinds of things—cups and glasses, and a pretty bowl from the top of the dinner table.

"I still don't see how it's right for him to take all those things," said Loudmouse to himself. "After all, he doesn't even live here."

At last the robber had put so much into his bag that there wasn't room for anything more. He set down the bag, walked into the kitchen, turned on the light, and started hunting for something to eat.

Loudmouse hopped after him and hid under a kitchen chair, where it was so dark that he could not be seen. When Loudmouse looked out from under the chair, what do you think he saw?

The man had cut a piece of the fine cheese,
and was about to eat it.

That was too much for Loudmouse.
He couldn't stand it. He *knew*
that the man had no right
to take that cheese.

ROBBer!

said Loudmouse,
more loudly than he had ever said anything.

WHAT MAKES YOU THINK THAT YOU CAN EAT OUR CHEESE ?

The robber gave a start, and his cap fell to the floor. He turned around to see who was there, and there was nothing to be seen.

This made him even more afraid, and so he ran as fast as he could to the living room and jumped right out the window, head first.

Loudmouse could hear Mr. and Mrs. Dowd talking to each other and getting out of bed. He picked up the piece of cheese which the robber had let fall, and ran back to his hole in the living room wall. When Mr. and Mrs. Dowd got down to the first floor, Mr. Dowd looked at the open window. Then he looked into the next room, and saw the bag on the floor.

Then he remembered Loudmouse's cry of "ROBBER!"
He turned to Mrs. Dowd and said, "Jane, I think that
we are going to be friends with that loud mouse, after all.
He has just stopped a robber from taking all our
best things."

Mrs. Dowd looked into the bag and said,
"Oh, my lovely bowl! And my cut-glass candlesticks!
And my gold box!

"To think that they'd all be gone,
if it hadn't been for that mouse!"

"It looks to me," said Mr. Dowd, "as if a watch mouse is
just as good as a watch dog. From now on I am going to be
very kind to that mouse, and make him feel right at home."

And that is just what he did.

From that time on, Mr. and Mrs. Dowd have left some
nice cheese in front of the mousehole every day.
Sometimes it is fine old cheese which has come by boat
from other lands. Loudmouse and his whole family eat
very well, and are right at home. And you may be sure
that Loudmouse keeps an eye out for robbers every night.

If you see a thing
Which is small in size,
With a tail that's long
And two bright eyes,
Which likes a bite
Of cheese at night
And makes more noise
Than a pair of boys,
Remember to sing
This remembering song,
And be very nice
To the best of mice.
You are looking at Loudmouse,
Who lives in the Dowd house.